A
JIGSAW
JO
MYST

The Case
of the
Vanishing
Painting

Read all the Jigsaw Jones Mysteries

And Don't Miss . . .

Coming Soon . . .

The Case of the Vanishing Painting

by James Preller
illustrated by Jamie Smith
cover illustration by R. W. Alley

A
LITTLE APPLE
PAPERBACK

SCHOLASTIC INC.
New York Toronto London Auckland Sydney
Mexico City New Delhi Hong Kong Buenos Aires

ISBN 0-439-66165-X

12 11 10 9 8 7   6 7 8 9/0

Printed in the U.S.A.   40
First printing, November 2004

*This book is dedicated to
Craig Walker,
for no reason at all.*

—JP

CONTENTS

Chapter One
Going Buggy

Helen Zuckerman waltzed into room 201 like a movie star. No, she wasn't sporting sunglasses or a mink coat. There were no bodyguards or flashing cameras. But Helen had something better. Something that turned her into an instant celebrity.

She wore a cast on her left arm.

Even better, she had a black eye.

The girls in the room quickly gathered around Helen, like bees buzzing around spring's first flower. Danika Starling grabbed

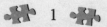 1

a marker. They all eagerly signed Helen's bright purple cast.

Clap, clap.

Automatically, the class responded to our teacher's signal. *CLAP, CLAP, CLAP.* All eyes turned toward Ms. Gleason.

"Good morning, boys and girls. Happy Monday," Ms. Gleason chimed. She looked at Helen and frowned. "Helen, dear, what in the world happened to you?"

Helen beamed. "I broke my arm in two places!"

The room filled with appreciative murmurs. Anybody can break an arm. But breaking it in two places — that took talent. Helen told us about her accident on the trampoline in her backyard. She did a flop when she meant to flip and went *boom* when she meant to zoom.

"Did it hurt very, very much?" asked Geetha Nair in her shy, quiet voice.

Helen grinned. "Sure, at first. But it

doesn't bother me now." Helen banged the cast on a desk. "Pretty cool, huh?"

We all agreed that "cool" was the best word to describe it. Except for Geetha, who seemed horrified and concerned.

"Don't sweat it, I'm fine," Helen insisted to Geetha. "No biggie."

We got started on our schoolwork. We did our morning sentences. That was when Ms. Gleason gave us two sentences that were all messed up. Words were misspelled. The punctuation was wrong. Names didn't have capital letters. Stuff like that. We fixed them up in a jiffy.

"Who is our ant monitor this week?" Ms. Gleason asked.

Stringbean Noonan's arm shot to the ceiling. I had to look twice to be sure it was still attached to his shoulder. "I am, I am, I am!" he cried.

You'd think Stringbean had won the lottery.

 4

But that was Stringbean. He was buggy about ants.

Not uncles. Not cousins or brothers. And not my Aunt Harriet, either. A-N-T-S. The six-legged kind.

Go figure.

Ms. Gleason had sent away for an ant farm at the beginning of the year. It arrived last week. Ever since, we'd been doing lots of ant activities. From science to math, it was all ants, all the time. Ant songs, ant math problems, ant books. It felt like we had ants crawling around inside our heads.

Ralphie Jordan joked, "If we're going to be farmers, I'm glad we're ant farmers. It beats growing cabbage!"

Ms. Gleason drew a picture of an ant on the chalkboard. "Ants are insects," she reminded us.

"And insects are our friends," Stringbean warmly added. "They live in communities and work together as a team!"

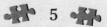

Ms. Gleason laughed. "Yes, they do, Jasper." (That's Stringbean's real name.)

Ms. Gleason labeled the ant's body parts — head, legs, antennae, thorax, and abdomen.

Ms. Gleason glanced at the wall clock. "Oh, my, look at the time. Clear your desks, boys and girls. Line up for art class. Mr. Manus will be out for another week. He's still on that African safari. Our visiting

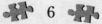

artist, Ms. Nicks, will be subbing again this week."

I glanced at Mila Yeh. She rolled her eyes and made a funny face. Mila is my best friend. A while back we started a detective business together. We've been partners ever since. We've found missing hamsters, dug up buried treasures, and hunted marshmallow monsters.

But Ms. Nicks was the strangest case we'd come across yet.

Chapter Two
What's That Smell?

Our whole class filed into the art room.

"Yuck, what's that smell?" Bobby Solofsky complained.

Joey Pignattano blushed. "Maybe it's me," he admitted. "I think I stepped in something on the way to school."

"It's not you, Joey," Mila said. "It's *that*."

Mila pointed to a wisp of smoke rising from a clay dish. The dish was in the palm of our substitute art teacher's hand.

"Jasmine incense," Ms. Nicks warbled. "It soothes the spirit and improves creativity."

"I don't know about that, Ms. Nicks," Joey replied. "But it sure does smell funny."

Ms. Nicks paid no attention. Instead, she glided across the room the way a breeze drifts across the tips of trees. Honest. Ms. Nicks didn't walk like other people. Instead, she sort of floated. Or it just looked that way because she wore such loose-fitting clothes, like robes and shawls and long scarves and flowing skirts. I never saw her feet. She could have had roller skates on, for all I know.

Nothing that Ms. Nicks did or said was ordinary.

Bigs Maloney had a word for it: "bonkers."

Mila thought she was funny. But not funny ha-ha. More like funny uh-oh.

Ms. Nicks fussed with a CD player. Soon, lazy music wafted through the air.

"I know this music," Kim Lewis exclaimed. "It's Yanni. My mom listens to it when she does yoga."

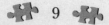

"Did someone say yogurt?" Joey asked hopefully. It was a typical Joey question. He was always thinking about food.

"Not yogurt, *Yanni*," Kim repeated. "He's like Raffi for old people who need to relax."

"I'm hungry," Joey grumbled.

Ms. Nicks pressed her palms together, closed her eyes, and began to hum. *Ommmmm.*

"Center your energies," Ms. Nicks whispered.

"Does that mean 'sit down'?" Eddie Becker asked.

"I think so," I replied.

We sat on the floor in a semicircle facing Ms. Nicks. It was how she made us start every art lesson. (Hey, I told you she was a strange case.)

Ms. Nicks took a deep breath. "Breathe in," she whispered. "Breathe out."

"Thanks for the reminder," Ralphie joked. "Solofsky was starting to turn blue."

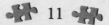 11

Some of us giggled. Ms. Nicks opened one eye. Her lips tightened. She shut her eye again. "Empty your minds of all thought," she whispered. *Ommmmm.*

Easy for her. I gave it a shot. But all I could think about was *not* thinking. I thought about jigsaw puzzles, and ants, and the itch on the tip of my nose.

"Don't even scratch," Ms. Nicks whispered. She looked at me with that one open eyeball again. "Just . . . BE."

 12

We sat there for what seemed like forever. Maybe it was only thirty seconds. But it felt like a long time. Finally, Ms. Nicks took an extra-loud breath, uncrossed her legs, and stood up. "Now we begin," she said.

Ralphie raised his hand. "Um, Ms. Nicks?"

"Yes, Mr. Jordan?"

"Before we get started," Ralphie said, "do you have an alarm clock? I think my foot's asleep."

Chapter Three
Playing with Ideas

I'll admit it. For all her weird ways, Ms. Nicks knew how to make art fun. She showed us work by lots of famous artists.

"Making art should be like play," Ms. Nicks told us. "Art is playing with ideas. Don't think too hard. Just . . . feel. And let yourself go!"

I buzzed in Mila's ear: "Earth to Ms. Nicks. Earth to Ms. Nicks. This is planet Earth calling. Please come home."

Mila giggled. By now we were all in our smocks, making a mess. Working on our projects, chattering and laughing. Having fun.

Ms. Nicks let us create whatever we wanted. She drifted around the room, humming to the music. Mila was making a papier-mâché sculpture, and a mess, but not in that order. Nicole Rodriguez was cutting up pieces of colored construction paper. Ms. Nicks gushed excitedly. She showed Nicole the artwork of Henri Matisse. He liked cutting up paper, too.

Last week, she had gotten Bigs Maloney excited about some artist's "paint splatter" approach. Bigs loved that. He set up his paper on the floor and gleefully dripped paint in big, sweeping motions. I think more of it got onto his shoes than on the paper, but Bigs didn't seem to mind.

Geetha was probably the best artist in our class. Not that she would ever admit it. Geetha is one of those quiet kids. Every class has one. Just shy, I guess.

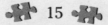

Anyway, I once talked her into helping out on a mystery. It was the case of the bicycle bandit. I brought Geetha with us to interview a witness. The witness, Mrs. Flint, described a boy on a skateboard, and Geetha drew a sketch of him. We made posters of the sketch, offering a reward, and hung them around town. In no time at all, we found the culprit, thanks to Geetha.

Geetha silently worked in the corner at

the big easel. She had it turned away from everyone, so I couldn't see what she was doing. But I'd bet it was pretty good.

Ralphie, on the other hand, had different ideas. I overheard him talking about his project with Joey.

"It's a collage," Ralphie explained. "A bunch of us are doing them. I'm putting all sorts of things in here that I like."

Joey leaned into the collage and frowned. "Is that chewing gum?" he asked.

"Not anymore," Ralphie said with a sly grin. "Now it's art!"

Joey was horrified. "It's not art," he protested. "It's a waste of good food!" Then he licked his lips. "Can I eat it?"

"No, you can't eat it!" Ralphie exclaimed. "It's ABC gum, Joey. It's Already Been Chewed!"

I was busy working on my own idea. I had drawn a big picture of myself. Then I cut up big jigsaw-shaped pieces of construction paper and glued the pieces

all over my self-portrait. Then I started drawing things that I liked, like baseball and pizza and detective work. It was fun.

During cleanup, Ms. Nicks told us some big news. "It's Parents' Night this Friday," she reminded us. "Mr. Rogers, the principal, has asked me to display your work in the main hallway." She blinked with enthusiasm. "Now everyone will see what wonderful artwork you've made!"

We all cheered. We were going to turn our school into a museum. And we were going to be the stars!

"Maybe my parents will buy my painting," Eddie Becker shouted, greedily rubbing his hands together. "I can get rich and retire early!"

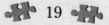

Chapter Four
Vanished!

Two days later, on Wednesday, we discovered that Geetha's painting was gone.

Vanished. Disappeared. Stolen.

That's bad news. But I'm a detective. Bad news is my business. When everybody's happy, I'm broke. That's just the way the world works.

Wednesday started out the same as any other day. Ms. Gleason reminded us that Parents' Night was in two days. She said,

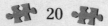

"I'm really looking forward to meeting your families."

I told her there wasn't much to get excited about. "Don't expect a lot. It's just my mom and dad," I said apologetically.

"Wait until you meet Bigs Maloney's dad," Joey said. "He's gigantic."

Bigs nodded proudly.

Ms. Gleason's eyes widened. "Well, Bigs. It will be fun watching your father try to sit in your chair."

"They sit in our chairs?" Danika asked.

"Some do," Ms. Gleason said. "You kids are welcome to come, too," she said. "Everyone's invited. It's just a friendly get-together."

We were all interested in the Parents' Night plans, but Stringbean couldn't stand it any longer. "Can we feed the ants now, PLEASE?"

Part of our ant project was to study and

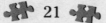 21

observe how the ants reacted to different kinds of foods. Every week we were going to experiment with something new, like grapes, salt, honey, bread crumbs, whatever.

"We'll feed the ants after lunch," Ms. Gleason answered Stringbean. "Right now, you've got a special class with Ms. Nicks. You don't usually have two art classes in one week, but we have to get ready for Parents' Night. I can't wait to see your work. Ms. Nicks is very impressed. I hope you'll all be proud to put it on display for everyone to see."

"You can buy my painting," Eddie Becker offered. He waved a price tag in the air. It read: $85 — CHEAP!

"Not on a teacher's salary," Ms. Gleason replied, perhaps a little sadly. "OK, boys

and girls. Off you go. While you're gone, I'll be sprucing up the bulletin board. I want room 201 to look awesome for your parents."

Ms. Nicks met us in the hallway. She was rushing to the art room and seemed out of breath. "I almost didn't get here in time," she said, huffing and puffing. "My unicycle had a flat tire."

The door to the art room was not locked. Ms. Nicks flicked on the lights. Our paintings and sculptures were drying on newspapers and easels. As Ms. Nicks fiddled with her beloved Yanni CD, I heard Helen exclaim, "Geetha? What's wrong?"

Geetha didn't answer. She stood staring at the corner easel. A few kids rushed over.

"Where's your painting?" Nicole asked.

The next few minutes were, in Ms. Nicks's words, "very stressful" and "full of negative energy."

They were not fun, that's for sure.

We looked up, down, and sideways for Geetha's painting. But we didn't find a trace of it.

"It couldn't have walked away by itself," Ms. Nicks said. She seemed very upset.

"Breathe," Helen reminded Ms. Nicks. "Feel centered. Think about your belly button. Just . . . BE."

Ms. Nicks sat down on the floor, closed her eyes, and hummed. *Ommmmm.*

Yeesh.

It was a mystery, all right. Ms. Nicks had said that Geetha's painting could not have walked away. But it had. Because somebody had walked away *with* it.

The question was: Who?

Chapter Five

The Gobstopper

Mila slipped me the secret signal. She slid a finger across her nose. "I'm on it," she whispered.

We didn't have time to sit around. We had to get back to room 201, grab our lunches, and head to the cafeteria.

That didn't stop a bunch of kids from telling Ms. Gleason about the missing painting. "I'm sure it will turn up," Ms. Gleason told Geetha kindly. "It must have been put aside by accident. I can't imagine that anyone would steal a painting."

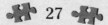

Geetha looked at her shoes and nodded. If she was upset, I couldn't tell. I don't think Geetha liked being the center of attention.

On the way to lunch, I slipped her my card:

NEED A MYSTERY SOLVED?
Call Jigsaw Jones
or Mila Yeh!
For a dollar a day,
we make problems go away.

CALL 555-4523 or 555-4374

Mila placed her hand on Geetha's. "We'll help find your painting, Geetha."

Geetha's lower lip trembled. She answered, "No . . . I . . . it's . . ."

"Is it money?" Mila asked. "We can work out a trade. You don't have to pay us right away."

That was news to me. I shot Mila the hairy eyeball.

Mila ignored me. Instead, she smiled at Geetha. "Let's talk in the cafeteria, OK?"

Geetha's eyes remained fixed on the floor. But her chin moved ever so slightly. A little nod. Yes.

We ate our lunches quickly.

I took out my detective journal. With a bright red marker, I wrote:

The Case of the Vanishing Painting

Mila began asking questions. "Tell us about your painting, Geetha."

Geetha looked at our faces. It was the first time I noticed the dark chocolate color of her eyes. Large and round. Here was a girl, I thought, who spent too much time looking at the floor.

"It was nothing," Geetha said. "Just a kind of painting and collage."

"Describe it," I said.

"Ms. Nicks said that I should use pieces of my life," Geetha explained.

"Huh?" I grunted.

Mila explained, "Jigsaw, when you make a collage, you're allowed to glue all sorts of different things onto the painting. It could be old photos, movie ticket stubs, candy wrappers, anything. Then you can go back and paint on top of them if you want to."

Geetha seemed relieved to have Mila speak for her.

"I need to hear it from you," I told

Geetha. "Was there anything in your artwork that was valuable? Was there anything in it that someone else would want?"

A new thought seemed to flicker in Geetha's eyes.

Her face turned pale.

"Yes," she whispered.

Over the next few minutes, Geetha explained her artwork down to the smallest detail. She even drew a sketch. As Mila had

guessed, Geetha had used several family photos in her painting. Plus some pink lace from her first ballet slippers. A friendship bracelet. Even a piece of her favorite candy, an Everlasting Gobstopper.

"What did you say?" I asked.

"A Gobstopper," Geetha repeated.

"You had candy stuck to the painting?"

Geetha seemed embarrassed. She brushed a strand of hair from her face. I took that as a yes.

My eyes scanned the cafeteria. I found our first suspect. He was stuffing a Twinkie into his mouth, sideways.

I wrote in my journal:

SUSPECTS
Joey Pignattano

We all knew that Joey would do almost anything for food.

I wondered if he'd steal for it.

Chapter Six
Spill It, Joey

I sat down across from Joey Pignattano.

"Hey, Jigsaw," he greeted me. "It's too bad about Geetha's painting. But you'll solve the mystery. You always do."

"Usually," I replied, "not always. You know we're friends, right, Joey?"

Joey slurped from a container of milk. A white mustache formed above his lip. "Sure we are. Why? Do you need a favor?"

"This is business," I replied. "I need to know the truth. Did you have anything to do with this vanishing painting?"

His fingers started tapping on the table. It wasn't a good sign. Joey looked away.

"No," Joey lied.

His fingers tapped faster, nervously.

"Geetha said she glued a piece of candy to her painting," I noted.

"I never touched that Gobstopper," Joey pleaded.

I sat back and crossed my arms. "Who said anything about a Gobstopper?"

"Um, you did." Joey paused, then doubtfully asked, "Didn't you?"

"I said it was candy," I replied. "I never told you it was an Everlasting Gobstopper."

Joey didn't answer. Which was probably a good idea, since he was a terrible liar. And that tells you a good thing about Joey Pignattano. Because if there's one thing I've learned in this line of work, it's this: The nicest people make the worst liars.

"Spill it," I demanded.

Joey's eyebrows arched. "What?"

 35

"You're holding out on me," I said. "You know something, and you're not telling. Go on," I urged. "Spill it."

"You want me to spill it?" Joey asked.

I should have noticed when his eyes went to the milk carton. But I didn't put two and two together fast enough. Because in the next instant, Joey reached across the table . . . and spilled the milk.

It oozed across the table. And right onto my lap!

I was a soggy detective. So I grumbled and groaned and wiped myself off. "I didn't mean spill the milk!" I complained. "I meant *spill it*. You know, tell me the truth!"

Joey's eyes widened. I could almost see the lightbulb turning on over his head. "Oh-ohh," he said.

After that, Joey confessed.

He didn't pocket the painting. But he did grab the Gobstopper.

I shook my head. "How could you?" I asked.

"How could I not?" Joey answered. "Those little suckers are delicious. It was like a little voice crying out to me: 'Eat me, Joey. Eat me. Eeeaaattt mmmeeee!'"

Oh, brother.

"You promise that you did not take the painting?" I asked.

"No way, Jigsaw," Joey promised.

I believed him. After all, why would Joey take a painting? He couldn't eat it.

"So . . . how was it?" I finally asked.

"How was what?"

"The Gobstopper."

"A little gluey," Joey admitted.

Suddenly, a chorus of voices filled the air. Mila and a bunch of other girls were standing around Geetha, singing. I knew the song. Ms. Gleason had taught it to us this week. It was part of our Insect Unit:

"Just what makes that little old ant
Think he'll move that rubber tree plant?
Anyone knows an ant can't
Move a rubber tree plant."

Helen was waving her cast around like an orchestra leader. Danika and Kim were swaying back and forth. Geetha sat in the center, watching them.

Then it really got loud:

"But he's got HIGH HOPES!
He's got HIGH HOPES . . ."

I watched Geetha's face. Slowly, the corners of her mouth lifted upward. She smiled. Then she joined in with her friends and quietly sang the rest of the song.

Chapter Seven

Detectives at Work

Have you ever tried to write while riding in the back of a school bus? *Bounce, bounce, scribble, rippp!* Yeesh.

I shut my detective journal. As Mila talked, I stared out the bus window with my chin in my hand.

The trees had dropped their leaves. Clear skies had turned gray. Songbirds had flown south. It suddenly hit me that we were driving into the long, cold, dark months of winter.

It made me feel blue.

"Jigsaw? Jigsaw? Are you even listening?"

It was Mila's voice. And no, I wasn't.

"What about Eddie Becker?" Mila repeated. "He's a suspect."

"How do you figure?" I asked.

"The oldest motive in the world," Mila answered. "Greed. Eddie loves money. Everybody knows that. Geetha is the best artist in the second grade. Maybe Eddie thought he could sell her painting."

I read my notes from our talk with

Geetha. "She mentioned there was a friendship bracelet in the collage," I said. "You think that's worth any money?"

Mila shook her head. "It's valuable because of what it *means,* not because of what it *costs*. It's probably just cheap beads and string."

"Could Ms. Nicks have stolen it?" I wondered. "We don't really know much about her."

Mila pulled on her long black hair.

"Doubtful," she concluded. "But Ms. Nicks was late getting to class. She'd been running. So I guess it's possible."

"Anything is possible," I commented. "But it's not likely. Still, now we know that Ms. Nicks had been away from the classroom. I remember that the door was not locked. That may have been the time of the robbery."

I closed my eyes and rested my head. For some reason, I felt incredibly tired. All I wanted to do was sleep.

I listened to the conversation behind me. Ralphie Jordan was complaining about our bus driver, Big Curtis.

"He never talks," Ralphie said. "Big Curtis just grunts. And nods. And frowns. But mostly, Big Curtis just scowls. He's, like, the worst bus driver in the whole school!"

"That's not true," Bobby Solofsky countered. "Big Curtis talks all the time."

Bobby imitated our bus driver's booming voice: "Sit down back there! Hurry up! Quiet down, you're giving me a *headache!*"

A few kids laughed. Bobby *did* sound like Big Curtis.

Mila turned around in her seat. "I think he's sweet," she said.

"Sweet?" Solofsky scoffed. "Maple syrup is sweet. Big Curtis is mean."

"No," Mila said. "He's . . . he's . . ." Mila searched for exactly the right word. "He's shy. That's why he doesn't seem friendly. Shy people do funny things. Deep down, I think Big Curtis is a big cream puff. Besides, it's his job to keep us safe. He has to yell."

"Whatever," Solofsky said. He buried his face in a SpongeBob SquarePants comic book.

Meanwhile, the wheels of the bus rolled round and round. And my mind whirred

like a broken clock. Who took Geetha's painting?

I didn't have a clue.

All I knew was that I felt very, very hot.

I suddenly realized why I felt so bad. I was getting sick.

Chapter Eight
Saved by the Bell

"Jigsaw, you look awful!" my mother exclaimed as I walked through the door.

I forced a grin. "It's nice to see you, too."

I plopped down on the couch. My mother felt my forehead and murmured concern. She said something about the twenty-four hour bug that was going around. Soon I was propped up with pillows and a blanket. There was a plate of toast that I didn't touch. I sipped ginger ale and tried to watch television.

I dozed for the rest of the day, on and off.

Sweating, achy, worn-out, and run-down. Some detective I turned out to be.

My mom didn't wake me on Thursday morning. I finally rose from bed to find my mother working on the computer. The rest of the house was quiet. No school for me.

Normally, I'd be happy to have a sick day. The problem is, sick days are wasted on the sick. I felt lousy. My brain wasn't working. I watched TV, ate soggy toast, and blobbed around. It wasn't exactly a thrill ride at Six Flags.

By two o'clock, I was feeling well enough to be bored, bored, bored.

"I'm bored," I grumbled to my mother. Then I said it again, a little louder. Maybe for the tenth time. In the last five minutes.

I think I may have been getting on my mom's nerves.

The first clue was when she gritted her teeth. Then she rubbed the temples of her head. My mother snapped, "Enough,

 49

Jigsaw! I know you haven't been feeling well. But you are really GETTING ON MY NERVES!"

You see, I'm a detective. I get paid to notice little things. And big things, too. Like, for example, the steam pouring out of my mom's ears.

"There's nothing to do," I pointed out.

"NOTHING TO DO? ARE YOU KIDDING?!"

"Mom," I said quietly, "maybe you should use your inside voice."

And maybe saying that wasn't such a good idea.

"How about this, Jigsaw?" she said. "There are puzzles to do, books to read, computer games to play. It seems to me that you're feeling a little better."

"But . . ."

"Find something to do," my mother said.

"But there isn't anything to do," I repeated.

Ding-dong. The doorbell rang.

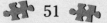 51

My mother smiled tightly. "Now there is," she said. "You can answer the door."

It was Mila. I think my mother was as happy to see her as I was. Mila unloaded a stack of board games on our living room table. Then she handed me a get-well card. It was written in code:

OHPE OYU RAE EFELIGN EBTTRE, EDTECTIEV!

"It's a twist code," Mila offered helpfully.

I remembered it from one of my code

books. If a word has two, three, or four letters, then you are supposed to switch the first two letters. So the word "SICK" becomes "ISCK."

But if a word is five letters or more, you flip-flop the first two and the last two letters. "BETTER" becomes "EBTTRE."

Pretty simple, once you get the hang of it. Mila had written:

HOPE YOU ARE FEELING BETTER, DETECTIVE!

And I was. I even ate a little something. Mila brought over all the ingredients. But it was Ms. Gleason's recipe. You just slather some cream cheese on a celery stalk. Then you drop on a row of raisins. Ants on a log!

"Thanks," I said while we played Checkers. "You're a good friend, Mila."

"That's what friends do," Mila answered. "They look out for each other."

Then she added seriously, "I've been thinking about the case, Jigsaw. Maybe Geetha stole her own painting."

Chapter Nine

The Suspect

You could have knocked me down with a feather boa.

"Geetha? Why do you suspect her?"

"She doesn't seem very upset," Mila said. "It's like she doesn't care."

"Geetha is quiet," I pointed out. "It's hard to tell what she's feeling."

Mila continued. "Other people seem more concerned about the painting than she does, though."

"Oh? Like who?"

"Helen, for example."

"Well, that makes sense," I countered. "Helen is Geetha's best friend."

"Yes," Mila agreed. "But Helen keeps asking me about the case. She wants to know if we've got any suspects yet."

"That's what friends are for," I said.

"There's more, Jigsaw," Mila said. "Something weird happened in school today. Ms. Nicks spoke to Geetha in the hallway. Luckily, I was on my way to the girls' room. So I stopped by the water fountain and took an extra-long drink."

I laughed. "And you listened while you drank!"

Mila's eyes twinkled. "Exactly. Pretty sneaky, huh? Anyway, Ms. Nicks wanted to hang another one of Geetha's pictures in the art display. But Geetha wouldn't let her."

"Really?"

"Geetha said that nothing else was good

enough. But I don't think that was really it," Mila said. "I think Geetha was happy she wasn't in the art show."

Mila knew more about girls than I did. She was usually right about these things. "I don't get it," I said. "Geetha's a great artist. You'd think she'd love to be the . . ."

". . . center of attention?" Mila filled in. "That's it, Jigsaw. Geetha is super-shy. She doesn't want anyone to notice her."

It was time for dinner. I walked Mila to the door. "Thanks for coming over," I said. "I'm feeling a lot better now. You're a good friend *and* a good detective."

"See you in school tomorrow?" Mila asked.

"Definitely," I replied. "We've got a mystery to solve. If Geetha did take this painting, we have to figure out how and when. You've already answered why."

My family was happy to see me back at the dinner table. For about ten seconds.

"I'm glad you're feeling better," Grams said. "Now pass the potatoes." For an old lady, Grams eats like a rhino.

"It's Parents' Night tomorrow," I reminded my parents.

"Wouldn't miss it for the world," my father murmured. "It would take wild horses to keep me away."

"We're looking forward to it," my mother quickly added. "We've heard a lot about Ms. Gleason. I can't wait to go through your folders to see what kind of work you've been doing."

"Through my folders?" I chirped.

"Yes," my mother answered. "We'll get to see all the things you've been doing in school."

"I'm not so sure I like this," I muttered.

During the rest of dinner, I kept thinking about Geetha. I wondered why someone would be that shy.

"We've got a girl in school," I began to tell my parents. "She's a great artist. But she's really, really shy. I don't think she wants to show her work in the art display."

"Yeah, so?"

That was my brother Nicholas.

My brother Daniel cared even less. He said, "Who cares?"

Yeesh.

"I care," my father chimed in pointedly.

I said to him, "You'd think that she'd *love* to show off her artwork."

"People are funny," my dad answered. "When you were little, I thought you'd love the circus. But you just cried and cried."

"Did not," I protested.

"Did, too," my sister Hillary said. She squealed in a high-pitched voice, "Momma, Dadda, the cwowns are scawing me!"

The cwowns?

"You were afraid of clowns," my father

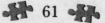 61

said. He shrugged, raising his palms in the air. "Who knew?"

"You must have me mixed up with some other guy," I scoffed. "What's for dessert?"

Chapter Ten

Crumbs

I was glad to get back to room 201 on Friday morning. I liked the usual hubbub before the morning bell sounded. Kids were pulling off backpacks and hanging jackets in cubbies. Joking and laughing, pushing and poking. Helen and Danika were performing magic tricks with Kim. Bobby and Bigs were arguing about something. Mila was talking with Geetha. It was good to be back.

Off by himself, Stringbean Noonan lay

sprawled on the floor. His nose was inches from the ant farm.

I sat beside him.

"Just look at them, Jigsaw," Stringbean marveled. "Ants are amazing."

"So are uncles," I joked.

It didn't get much of a laugh. But it wasn't much of a joke, either.

"Have you ever noticed that ants are just like people?" Stringbean said. "They live together. They work together. Just look at this little guy."

 64

Stringbean pointed to an ant that was struggling to carry a crumb. "Can you imagine how heavy that little crumb must be for him? It's like you or me trying to carry a school bus."

Another ant came along to help out. Together they carried that crumb deeper into a tunnel. "Those are the worker ants," Stringbean noted. "See how they help each other? Ants may be small, but they work together to solve big problems."

He paused. "We can all learn a lot from our friends in the insect world."

I'm not kidding. That's really how he talked.

I wouldn't make this stuff up.

A huge roar of laughter suddenly filled the room. Helen had tricked Danika by making a pen disappear. Then, presto, Helen revealed her secret. She had hidden the pen in her sling!

"What a great hiding spot!" Kim declared.

Yes, it sure was.

I pulled out my detective journal and started scribbling.

Mila came over. "What's going on, Jigsaw? Have you figured something out?"

"Helen's sling!" I exclaimed. "I may have figured out the HOW."

"What?"

"HOW," I repeated. "Not what. And WHO, too. Helen might be the thief! If she can make pens disappear, maybe she can make paintings vanish."

Mila rocked back and forth, thinking.

"OK, Jigsaw. Let's say that maybe, just maybe, Helen did hide the painting in her sling. I suppose she could have rolled it up and put it in there. But WHY?"

"You said it yourself at my house yesterday," I told Mila. "Friends look out for each other."

"Yeah, so?"

"So add it up," I replied. "Helen is best friends with Geetha. Helen knows that Geetha is shy. She knows that Geetha wouldn't want to display her artwork for everyone to see."

I continued excitedly. "Stringbean was talking about ants. He said that ants were just like people." I double-checked my notes. "Stringbean said, 'They help each other out.'"

Mila broke into a smile. "Helen made the painting disappear, just like in that magic trick."

"And she did it," I said, "because she was trying to help a friend."

Mila punched me in the shoulder. "I think you might be on to something."

"We still need proof," I said, rubbing my shoulder. "Have you signed Helen's cast yet?"

"Yes, all the girls have."

"Rats and snails. OK then, I guess I'll have to sign it," I decided.

"Why?" Mila asked.

"I need to get a look inside that sling," I told Mila. "If Helen hid the painting in her sling, I'd bet my last magnifying glass that some of the paint rubbed off."

Chapter Eleven
Parents' Night

Mila and I cornered Helen out on the playground during recess. I asked to sign her cast, peeked inside the sling, and there they were. Just as I had suspected.

Paint smudges.

"Hmmm," I murmured. "I wonder how that got there?"

I looked Helen in the eye.

"Sloppy painter, I guess," she explained.

"On the inside of your sling?" Mila asked pointedly.

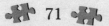

We told Helen what we thought. That she had taken the painting, and why she had taken it. "You were trying to protect a friend," I said. "I understand that. But I think you did the wrong thing."

Helen didn't deny it.

"That's why you kept asking me about the case," Mila said. "You were worried that we might figure it out."

Helen frowned. "Things didn't work out like I planned," she groaned.

Mila spoke up. "If you are willing, Helen, we just might have a better idea."

It was Parents' Night. And our plan was set. We just needed to cross our fingers and hope. Well, maybe we needed to cross our toes, too.

I drove to the school with my parents and my brother Nicholas, who was in fifth grade. We had to park two blocks away because the parking lot was full. Inside, the school was a mob scene. It was strange to see so many big people in the halls. Everything seemed much smaller than usual.

My parents went to Nick's classroom first. The fifth-grade rooms were on the other side of the building. "I'll wait in the cafeteria," I told them. The PTA was raising money with a bake sale. I thought I'd help them out by buying a couple of cupcakes. "Have you got a dollar?" I asked my dad.

Then I went to find Mila in the cafeteria.

She was already chatting with Helen and Geetha. "Did you tell her yet?" I asked Helen.

Helen gulped. Then she told Geetha about how she "stole" the painting.

"I didn't plan it," Helen explained. "The art room was open. So I went in and rolled up your painting. I hid it in my sling, then stuffed it in my cubby when everyone was outside for recess."

Geetha was confused. And, as usual, very quiet.

"I did it for you," Helen explained to Geetha. "I knew you didn't want to show your painting in the art show."

Geetha studied the tops of her feet. Her head bobbed up and down in agreement.

"Helen brought the painting with her," Mila said hopefully. "I have some tape. We could still hang it up with everybody else's."

Geetha glanced briefly at Mila. "No," she whispered. "Don't do that."

"Geetha," I said, "you have so much talent. I think you're a great artist."

"You do?"

"Everybody does," Mila said.

"Jigsaw and Mila are right," Helen urged. "You have a special talent, Geetha. You should be proud of it. Come on. I'm your best friend in the world. Would I steer you wrong?"

Geetha's mouth twitched, as if it were deciding what to do.

"Trust me," Helen said. "Don't be shy. Just this once, let all these people, and your parents, see what great work you do."

The corners of Geetha's mouth lifted slightly. Finally, she agreed.

In a flash, we unrolled Geetha's painting and hung it with all the others. The art show was amazing. It took up the whole hallway leading to the gym.

"Yours is the best one," I told Geetha.

She looked at me with those chocolate brown eyes and said, "Thank you, Jigsaw."

We rushed back to room 201. Ms. Gleason was moving around the room, talking to different parents. Joey was right; it was funny to see big Mr. Maloney sitting in a kid-sized chair. Stringbean Noonan was showing the ant farm to his parents. Danika's folks were leafing through her writing journal, smiling and proud. Joey Pignattano, of course, was snarfing down a brownie.

And nobody bought Eddie Becker's painting. I guess the price was too high — by about $84.50.

Go figure.

Another mystery was solved. "This was a good case," Mila said to me. "Everyone raved about Geetha's painting." She nodded to Geetha, who was laughing with some other kids. "I think she's happy."

I thought so, too.

I guess that happy endings aren't just for fairy tales and children's books. Sometimes they happen in real life. Like right here, today, in room 201. With the help of some good detective work. If I do say so myself.

About the Author

James Preller often draws upon his own life as a basis for his Jigsaw Jones books. Like Jigsaw, James Preller has a slobbering, sock-eating dog. Like Jigsaw, James was the youngest in a large family. His older brothers called him Worm and worse — yeesh! And so do Jigsaw's!

James and Jigsaw both love jigsaw puzzles, baseball, grape juice, and mysteries! But even though Jigsaw and James have so much in common, they are not the same person.

Unlike Jigsaw, James Preller is the author of more than 80 books for children, including *The Big Book of Picture-Book Authors & Illustrators; Wake Me in Spring; Hiccups for Elephant;* and *Cardinal & Sunflower.* He lives outside of Albany, New York, with his wife, Lisa, three kids — Nicholas, Gavin, and Maggie — his cat, Blue, and his dog, Seamus.

A JIGSAW JONES MYSTERY

Here's a sneak peek at the next

#26 The Case of the Double Trouble Detectives

by James Preller

Top Secret

The Detective Journal of Jigsaw Jones, Private Eye

Case: The Case of the Double Trouble Detectives

Client: Mike Radcliffe

There's a new detective in town. And two detectives are double trouble! But Reginald Pinkerton Armitage III is nothing like Jigsaw. He uses fancy gadgets to get his work done. Gadgets don't make the detective, and Jigsaw is determined to prove it.

Is Jigsaw's town big enough for two Private Eyes? It's time for a showdown. May the best detective win!

Jigsaw and his partner, Mila, know that mysteries are like jigsaw puzzles—you've got to look at all the pieces to solve the case!

____	0-590-69125-2	#1: The Case of Hermie the Missing Hamster	$3.99 US
____	0-590-69126-0	#2: The Case of the Christmas Snowman	$3.99 US
____	0-590-69127-9	#3: The Case of the Secret Valentine	$3.99 US
____	0-590-69129-5	#4: The Case of the Spooky Sleepover	$3.99 US
____	0-439-08083-5	#5: The Case of the Stolen Baseball Cards	$3.99 US
____	0-439-08094-0	#6: The Case of the Mummy Mystery	$3.99 US
____	0-439-11426-8	#7: The Case of the Runaway Dog	$3.99 US
____	0-439-11427-6	#8: The Case of the Great Sled Race	$3.99 US
____	0-439-11428-4	#9: The Case of the Stinky Science Project	$3.99 US
____	0-439-11429-2	#10: The Case of the Ghostwriter	$3.99 US
____	0-439-18473-8	#11: The Case of the Marshmallow Monster	$3.99 US
____	0-439-18474-6	#12: The Case of the Class Clown	$3.99 US
____	0-439-18476-2	#13: The Case of the Detective in Disguise	$3.99 US
____	0-439-18477-0	#14: The Case of the Bicycle Bandit	$3.99 US
____	0-439-30637-X	#15: The Case of the Haunted Scarecrow	$3.99 US
____	0-439-30638-8	#16: The Case of the Sneaker Sneak	$3.99 US
____	0-439-30639-6	#17: The Case of the Disappearing Dinosaur	$3.99 US
____	0-439-30640-X	#18: The Case of the Bear Scare	$3.99 US
____	0-439-42628-6	#19: The Case of the Golden Key	$3.99 US
____	0-439-42630-8	#20: The Case of the Race Against Time	$3.99 US
____	0-439-42631-6	#21: The Case of the Rainy Day Mystery	$3.99 US
____	0-439-55995-2	#22: The Case of the Best Pet Ever	$3.99 US
____	0-439-55996-0	#23: The Case of the Perfect Prank	$3.99 US
____	0-439-55998-7	#24: The Case of the Glow-in-the-Dark Ghost	$3.99 US
____	0-439-66165-X	#25: The Case of the Vanishing Painting	$3.99 US

Super Specials

____	0-439-30931-X	#1: The Case of the Buried Treasure	$3.99 US
____	0-439-42629-4	#2: The Case of the Million-Dollar Mystery	$3.99 US
____	0-439-55997-9	#3: The Case of the Missing Falcon	$3.99 US

Available wherever you buy books, or use this order form.

Scholastic Inc., P.O. Box 7502, Jefferson City, MO 65102

Please send me the books I have checked above. I am enclosing $_____ (please add $2.00 to cover shipping and handling). Send check or money order—no cash or C.O.D.s please.

Name _____ Age _____

Address _____

City _____ State/Zip _____

Please allow four to six weeks for delivery. Offer good in the U.S. only. Sorry, mail orders are not available to residents of Canada. Prices subject to change.

SCHOLASTIC and associated logos are trademarks and/or registered trademarks of Scholastic Inc.

JJBL1004